This book belongs to

_____

VOLUME
17

# DONALD
# LEARNS A LESSON

## WALT DISNEY FUN-TO-READ LIBRARY

## A BANTAM BOOK
### TORONTO • NEW YORK • LONDON • SYDNEY • AUCKLAND

ISBN 0-553-05596-8

Published simultaneously in the United States and Canada.   Bantam Books are published by Bantam Books, Inc.   Its
trademark, consisting of the words "Bantam Books" and the portrayal of a rooster, is Registered in U.S. Patent and
Trademark Office and in other countries.   Marca Registrada.   Bantam Books, Inc., 666 Fifth Avenue, New York,
New York 10103.   Printed in the United States of America   0 9 8 7 6 5 4 3 2 1

Donald was dreaming he was on a boat sailing out to sea. All at once he heard a noise. *Thump, thump, thump, thump.* What was that?

Donald opened his eyes. He was in his
own bed in his own room. The sun was
shining. The noise was coming from outside.

He rolled over and looked out the window.
The thumping noise was the sound of Daisy
running. And Huey, Dewey, and Louie were
following her.

"Daisy does nothing but run anymore," said Donald. "She never has time to visit with me. I think I'll have a talk with her." So he got dressed and went outside.

Donald could see that Huey, Dewey, and Louie thought Daisy was wonderful. She could run fast and she could run far.

"Gee, Aunt Daisy. You're really strong," said Huey.

"We want to be strong like you," said Dewey and Louie.

"Now listen," said Donald. "You don't have to run to be strong. I am strong too."

"Not as strong—" said Huey.

"—as Aunt Daisy," said Louie.

"She keeps fit," said Dewey.

"Ha!" said Donald. "Who needs all that fitness stuff? I don't."

But Daisy and the boys kept running on their way.

Later that day Donald went for a walk. He had not gone far when he heard something. *Boing! . . . Boing! . . . Boing!* What was that noise?

He followed the sound. It got louder. *BOING! . . . BOING! . . . BOING!* He followed it into Daisy's yard.

Daisy was jumping on her trampoline.
Higher and higher she jumped. Then she did
a back flip.

"Great!" called Huey, Dewey, and Louie.
They clapped and cheered.

"Huey, Dewey, and Louie think you are pretty strong," said Donald. "But I am stronger than you are. I can show you that!"

"Oh, good," said Daisy. "Let's have a contest. How about a bicycle race next week?"

"Sure," said Donald. "That's easy. And let's have a trampoline contest too!"

"But you have never done that," said Daisy. "I don't think you should go on the trampoline, Donald."

"Well, I do!" said Donald. "We will see who is best on the trampoline. Then we will have a bicycle race."

"Okay, Donald," Daisy said with a smile.
And she began to work out. She exercised
all the rest of that day.

Donald did not want to work out. "Who needs all that fitness stuff? What I need is lots of rest."

Resting was what Donald did best. He made sure he got plenty of it!

Huey, Dewey, and Louie told Donald how much Daisy was preparing for the contest.

"She can jump rope for an hour—without stopping for a rest!" said Louie.

"She can do 100 push-ups in a row!" said Huey.

"She can run faster and farther than anyone," said Dewey.

"That does not mean she can beat <u>me</u> in a race!" said Donald with a laugh.

Huey, Louie, and Dewey told Daisy what Donald had said.
She smiled and just kept working out.

Daisy ran five miles every morning. She
swam 50 laps every day.

Daisy ate all the right things. She wanted
to be ready for her contest with Donald.

Soon there were only two days until the contest. Donald watched Daisy as she ran by his window.

"I guess it would not hurt to work out for a little while," he said.

Donald looked at himself in the mirror.
"Stomach in, chest out! Just look at all these
muscles. Daisy does not stand a chance!"

"Well, what should I do first?" Donald asked himself. "I think I'll try running. It couldn't be too hard!"

Donald counted as he ran, "One. Two. Three. Four. And one. Two. Three. Four." He held his head up high. "This is easy. I could run like this for hours."

But soon he began to huff and puff. "Oh, boy," he said. "It seems like a long way home. It didn't seem this far before!" He ran slower and slower. And he huffed and he puffed even more.

At last he got home. He sat down to
rest. "I'll just take a short nap," he thought.
But Donald slept for the rest of that day.
He slept all that night, too!

The next day Donald got up and stretched his arms out wide. "Ouch, that hurts! It sure is hard to move!" he said. "I had better exercise a little more, to get my muscles going!"

He touched his toes. One. Two. Three.
Four. And one. Two. Three. Four.
"That's enough of those," he thought.

He did push-ups. One. Two. Three.
"That seems like enough to me!"

All that work had made Donald hungry. "I
had better eat to keep up my strength," he said.
"Tomorrow is going to be a big day."
    Eating was something that Donald did well.
So he made sure he ate plenty!

Now it was the morning of the contest.
Of course, Donald woke up late. He hurried
into his clothes.

He ran all the way to Daisy's house.
Daisy and the nephews were waiting
for him.

Daisy was ready to start the contest.
"Would you like to be the first on the trampoline?" she asked.
"Ladies first!" said Donald.

Up Daisy went. She jumped once. She jumped twice. She jumped higher and higher. Then she began to flip over and over. She flipped and flipped until Donald grew dizzy. Then she jumped neatly off the trampoline.

"Hurray for Daisy!" cried Huey, Dewey, and Louie.

"Watch this," said Donald. He climbed up on the trampoline. He jumped once. He jumped twice. He jumped higher and higher, and higher and higher.

"Look out, Uncle Donald," cried Huey, Dewey, and Louie.

Donald never got to do a flip. He landed in a tree instead.

"Don't worry, Uncle Donald. We'll get you down." The nephews helped him out of the tree.

Donald brushed himself off. "Well, never mind the trampoline!" he said. "I know I will win the bicycle race."

"We'll see," said Daisy. "Are you sure you are ready? You seem a bit tired."

"Just you wait, Daisy. You won't even be able to keep up!" said Donald.

They took their places on their bicycles. The race was about to begin.

"On your mark. Get set. And go!"
shouted Huey.

"Last one around the block is a sore
loser," cried Daisy. And with that, she raced
past Donald in a flash.

Donald huffed. Donald puffed. He just
could not keep up. Soon Daisy could not be
seen. Donald's legs were beginning to hurt.

At last Donald got back to Daisy's house. There stood Daisy. And she looked fresh as a daisy!

But Donald looked very tired. "Daisy, you won, fair and square," he said sadly. "I was not ready for this race. And you were!"

"I guess—" said Huey.
"—it pays—" said Dewey.
"—to be prepared!" shouted Louie.
"Yes," said Donald, "it certainly does!"